THE
CREEPY
CLASSICS

CHILDREN'S
COLLECTION

Published by Sweet Cherry Publishing Limited, 2024
Unit 36, Vulcan House, Vulcan Road,
Leicester LE5 3EF, United Kingdom

Nauschgasse 4/3/2 POB 1017
Vienna, WI 1220, Austria

SWEET CHERRY and associated logos are trademarks and/or
registered trademarks of Sweet Cherry Publishing Limited.

2 4 6 8 10 9 7 5 3 1

ISBN: 978-1-78226-381-4

The Creepy Classics Children's Collection:
The Fall of the House of Usher

Text based on the original story by Edgar Allan Poe,
adapted by Gemma Barder
Illustrations by Nick Moffatt

www.sweetcherrypublishing.com

Printed and bound in India

THE FALL OF THE HOUSE OF USHER

EDGAR ALLAN POE

Sweet
Cherry

RODERICK USHER

A strange and
haunted young man

MADELINE USHER

Roderick's sister

THE NARRATOR

Roderick's childhood friend

CHAPTER ONE

The House of Usher was bleak,
cold and unwelcoming, like a
mansion of gloom. I saw the
place from at least a mile away
as I rode towards it on horseback.
The house stood lonely and isolated
on the top of a hill, and as soon as
I glimpsed it, I felt an icy shiver
run down my spine. It was as if a
cloak of misery had wrapped itself
around me which I was unable to
shake off. The grand, grey stone

building with black roof tiles
seemed to give off an air of sadness.
Even from this distance, I could see
the bleak walls, and the unseeing
eyes of the windows. Trails of green
ivy and moss seemed to creep up
every surface. I slowed my horse
and reached into the

pocket of my jacket to double-check the directions my friend, Roderick, had given me. Sure enough, it was the right house.

As I approached, the evening light seemed to give the house an eerie glow. I shuddered and quickly dismounted before making my way through a gothic archway into the courtyard. On one side of the house there was a steep bank of trees, and on the other, a black lake stretched out into the distance.

Roderick Usher had been my friend since we were at boarding school together. He was a pale, quiet boy who struggled to make friends, but for some reason the two of us got along. As the first school year went by, Roderick seemed to come out of his shell a little. He joined in with games, studied hard and laughed more often. When he returned to school after the summer holidays, however, he seemed to go back to his shy, nervous ways. He was reserved, as though there was always something else on his mind.

After our schooldays ended and we went our separate ways, we wrote to each other for a little while. I had not seen or heard from him for many years until a few weeks ago, when I received a letter from him.

My dear friend,

I would be very grateful if you could find the time to visit me at my home, the House of Usher (directions included), I have not felt very well lately, and I remember that you were always someone who could bring me out of my shell and cheer me up. It would be my pleasure to have you stay with me for one week if you have the time. Please write and let me know if you can come.

Your faithful friend,
Roderick Usher

He enclosed a set of directions, and, as I had nothing particularly urgent to do that week, I happily wrote back accepting his offer to come and stay.

I had to admit, I often thought about Roderick and wondered how he was getting on in the world. I knew very little about his life at home and I could not picture him away from school.

It worried me to hear that he was not well, but I was confused too. Roderick did not say *what* he was suffering from. Was it a physical sickness or an illness of the mind? Nor did I know if anyone was looking after him.

I had read in the papers that his parents had died some years earlier. There were rumours that no one from the Usher family ever flourished; from generation to generation, only one member of the family survived.

I sighed as I took in the dreary, dull house one more time, before heading towards the front door.

flourished
To do well, thrive or be successful.

CHAPTER TWO

Up close, the House of Usher
looked no better than it had from
afar. In fact, if anything, it was
worse. Moss and ivy covered the
outside, hanging in tangled webs
from the roof and windows. The
driveway was lined with the bare,
white trunks of long, dead trees.
Whoever the gardener was,
I would advise Roderick to find
a different one. Everything looked
old, unloved and in a state of

decline. It was almost as if the house itself had absorbed the disease from the decaying trees and the murky pond.

As I looked closer, I could barely believe my eyes. There

seemed to be a crack in the middle of the house, right through the stonework. It stretched all the way from the pitch of the roof down to the right-hand side of the house where the property met the edge of the lake. It was as if the house was decaying right in front of me.

I was just reaching out to touch it when a stable boy appeared out of nowhere.

'May I take your horse, sir?' he said politely, his hand outstretched for the reins.

I thanked him and passed over my horse. I was then greeted at the door by an ancient-looking butler who stared at me solemnly. He was tall and skinny with only a few wisps of silver hair around his ears. His skin tone matched the grey walls of the house almost identically.

'I am here to see Mr Usher,

Roderick,' I said cheerfully. 'I have been invited to stay.'

The old butler nodded wordlessly and turned around. I followed him inside the gloomy house as he took a candle from the table by the door. Although it was only just evening, there was no natural light inside the corridors of the house. No welcoming reception parlour, no sweeping staircase. Just dark, narrow corridors to be trudged through as I followed the silent butler. The house was as gloomy on the inside as it was on the outside. I could

almost feel its misery pressing down on me.

Hanging on the walls were portraits that seemed to stare down at me, accusingly. Next to them were landscapes of the house, painted from different directions.

There were carvings on the ceiling, suits of armour stood in the shadows and the floors were an unforgiving black.

Eventually, I saw another

person. It was a doctor coming down the stairs we were now climbing. The butler ignored him, and I would have laughed out loud at his rudeness, had the doctor not stared at me and shaken his head slightly, as if to say that he was used to the old butler's ways. 'Good evening,' he said politely as we passed each other.

Finally, we stopped outside a dark wooden door. The butler

opened it and stood aside, waiting for me to go in. 'Thank you,' I said to the butler. 'You have been most helpful.'

The butler nodded once, then walked away, taking the candle with him.

'Roderick?' I said, stepping inside what appeared to be a large studio. There were tall, thin windows at the far end of the room that let in a shard of fading sunlight, but otherwise there was no light aside from a small lamp on the desk and the glow of the fireplace. Dark draperies

hid the walls, and every piece of furniture looked uncomfortable, tattered and old. A stack of paperwork was piled up on the desk, and the floor was littered with books and musical instruments. Suddenly, to my amazement, the cluttered heap on the desk began to move.

CHAPTER THREE

The pile of clutter revealed itself to be my old friend, Roderick Usher.

'You came!' Roderick cried, rising up from the desk where he had been laying his head.

'I wrote to tell you I was coming,' I said. 'Did you get the letter?'

Roderick looked helplessly around the desk and shuffled some of the papers around him. 'I– it must be here somewhere,' he replied. 'Never mind, my friend.

You are here now and that is all that matters.'

He moved around the desk and strode towards me through the gloom. As he walked, I was struck by how thin and frail he was.

His clothes hung off his skeletal figure and he dragged his feet behind him in an unnatural manner. Before I could say anything, he threw his arms around me and hugged me tightly. When he pulled away, I could see that there was no doubt about his poor health. In fact, I would not have recognised him as the boy I went to school with had I not been standing in his own house.

Roderick Usher was ghostly white. His large, blue eyes were

skeletal
To be like a frame of bones.

circled with dark rings and his lips were horribly pale. His fair hair drooped around his face, and it was clear it had not been cut for many weeks. Thin, patchy stubble lined his face and made him look older than his years.

Seeing the shocked look on my face, Roderick stood back and looked a little embarrassed. 'I am sorry for my appearance,' he said. 'I haven't had much company apart from some doctors, and I was not sure if you would come.'

It was clear my friend had not been expecting me. My letter was no doubt lost in the chaos on his desk and I felt sad that Roderick had got himself into such a sorry state.

I smiled gently, taking in his creased shirt and trousers. They looked as if they had seen better days. 'What does that matter between old friends?' I said. 'I am glad to see that you are up and about and not in bed.'

Roderick ran a hand through his hair nervously. 'I was just about to get myself dressed,' he laughed, as if trying to make light of the situation. 'Would you like

some tea? Or something to eat?
You must have had a long journey.'

'Tea would be lovely,' I said.
'Shall we sit by the fire?'

The fireplace was a welcoming
spot in the gloomy room. The fire
was fading, so before I sat down,
I threw some kindling and a few
of the driest-looking logs on top.

The old butler entered with a tray of tea things. He placed it down on the table closest to us and left without saying a word. Silence filled the room.

'In your letter you told me you were ill,' I said at last. 'Is there anything I can help you with to ease your symptoms?'

Roderick looked at me. For a moment, he looked terrified, then he turned to face the fire. 'I hope so,' he said quietly. 'I remember at school you could always make me feel better.'

'That's kind of you to say,' I said.

'But I am not a doctor.'

'Doctors can't help me,' Roderick growled, and another silence fell between us. 'I'm sorry, old friend,' he said eventually. 'It's just that I have seen so many doctors, and none of them believe what I have to say.'

I placed my teacup gently back on the tray and sat back in my chair. The warmth of the fireplace made me feel more relaxed than I had been since I first stepped into the house. 'Can you tell me about it?' I asked. 'I promise I will believe you.'

Chapter Four

Roderick leant forwards in his chair and rested his arms on his knees. I could see the thinness of his limbs through his clothes. 'It is a family illness,' Roderick began. 'Both my parents died of it, and I am terrified that Madeline will die of it too and leave me all alone.'

For a moment I did not know who he was talking about, then I remembered that Roderick had a sister. I wondered where she could be and if she still lived in the house.

'We are the last of the Ushers, you see, Madeline and I,' Roderick said, tears welling in his eyes. 'There are no aunts or uncles or cousins. When we pass away, the house and everything in it will be gone. It has been in our family for hundreds of years, and yet ...' Roderick covered his face with his hands, unable to continue.

I reached over and placed a hand on my friend's arm to try

and comfort him. 'What exactly *is* the illness that has affected your family so terribly?' I asked.

'There is no name for it,' Roderick said breathlessly, shaking his head. 'I just can't seem to quieten my mind and all my senses seem to be heightened. I can smell the dust of the road on your jacket. I can only wear the clothes I have on now, as everything else seems to scratch and irritate my skin. I can't stand any music, apart from when it is played on a stringed instrument, and I feel afraid all the time.'

Roderick paused and looked me square in the eyes. 'You think I am crazy, don't you?'

I shook my head. 'No,' I said, quickly reassuring him. 'Of course not. I think you are tired and stressed and in need of comfort – that is why I have come.'

Roderick smiled and breathed a little easier. He stared at the fire once more.

'Do you know *what* might be causing you to feel the way you do? Do the doctors have any ideas at all?' I asked, gently. Roderick looked fearfully from side to side, almost as if he was afraid of being overheard.

'The doctors know nothing, but of course, *I* know the reason,' he whispered. 'It is this house. This house is killing me one day at a time and there is no escape.'

I did not know what to say. Certainly, the house was not a pleasant place to be. It felt damp and cold, even with the fire burning brightly beside us, but I did not think it was bad enough to kill anyone. 'Perhaps you could make some improvements?' I suggested. 'Remove the moss and the ivy? Repair the crack?'

Roderick stared at me wildly. 'You do not understand!' he cried. 'This house, this place, it has a power you can only dream of.' Before he could say anything further, a door opened at the far end of the room and a small glow cast a weak light into the room. The light was coming from a lamp, held by a young woman.

CHAPTER FIVE

The young woman walked into the room as though she were sleepwalking. For a moment, I thought she was a ghost and felt horribly afraid. She was dressed in a long, flowing nightgown and her hair was loose. She was so thin that she seemed to be

wasting away. It was only when she spoke to Roderick that I snapped out of my own trance.

'I am going to bed, brother,' she said simply, without acknowledging me. 'I am so tired. Do not keep me awake with your ranting and raving again.'

With that, she left the room. I looked at Roderick to see that he was teary-eyed. 'You must excuse Madeline,' he said. 'She is not well either. She suffers from dreadful fits and seizures. They

seizures
A very sudden attack of an illness where someone becomes unconscious or develops violent movements.

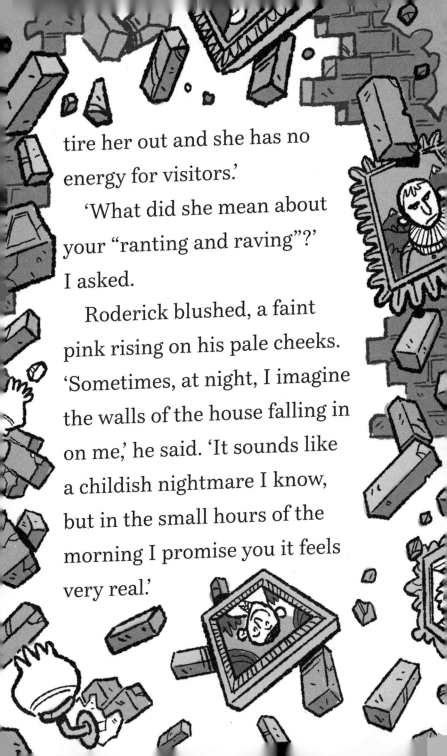

tire her out and she has no energy for visitors.'

'What did she mean about your "ranting and raving"?' I asked.

Roderick blushed, a faint pink rising on his pale cheeks. 'Sometimes, at night, I imagine the walls of the house falling in on me,' he said. 'It sounds like a childish nightmare I know, but in the small hours of the morning I promise you it feels very real.'

I believed Roderick and I was starting to remember why we had been such good friends at school. He was interesting and honest, and so different to the rest of the boys we grew up with. I felt protective of him, even now, all these years later. 'I have an idea,' I said. 'Why don't we ask your butler to set me up with a bed in your room? It will be just like when we shared a dorm at school. Then, if you wake in the night and feel scared or imagine the walls are falling down, I will be there.'

Roderick gave me a genuine

smile, for the first time since my arrival. 'I think that sounds just splendid,' he said, ringing the bell for the butler to pass on our plans.

***

Roderick's room was large enough for a small bed to be carried in and placed at the foot of his own grand four-poster. If I was being completely honest, I was glad not to be in a room on my own. The house unsettled me, and I was happy to have my friend close, even if I was the one who was supposed to be supporting him.

We changed into our pyjamas and discussed what we would do in the week ahead. Roderick was keen to stay inside and dismissed any ideas I had of walking the grounds. When I asked about the gardener, Roderick said that they

had not had one since his parents died. When I suggested fishing on the lake, his face almost turned grey, and he shook his head without speaking. Instead, Roderick wanted to show me his books and talk of old times. I agreed, hoping it would help build up his spirits.

'Perhaps Madeline might join us?' I said, as I blew out the candle by my bed.

'I don't think so,' Roderick answered. 'She keeps to her room

most of the time.
I should let you
know that the
doctors do not
think she will
recover
from her fits.

I hope they are wrong.'

With that sad thought in mind,
we said goodnight.

CHAPTER SIX

The following morning, Roderick woke in a brighter mood. We ate breakfast in the dining room, and I noticed that the curtains on one side of the room were still closed.

'Would you like me to let some light in, Roderick?' I asked, getting up from my seat.

Roderick shook his head forcefully. 'I prefer those windows to remain covered, actually,' he said in a tone that allowed

no argument. 'Now, if you will
excuse me, I am going to look in
on Madeline.' Roderick gave me
a quick smile and left me on my
own. I listened to his footsteps
fading away along the corridor,
then quickly got up and took my
cup of tea to the curtains. With a
quick look around to make sure
the silent butler was nowhere to
be seen, I peeked behind them.
Through the window I could see
a magnificent view of the lake at
the side of the house. The morning
sun glistened on the water, and
I imagined having breakfast in

this room with the curtains wide open, taking in the view and the horizon beyond. It was obvious the room had been designed with that in mind.

It occurred to me that Roderick was frightened of the lake. Perhaps he had had a bad experience and was afraid of being reminded of it. As I continued to take in the view, I felt myself drawn to the water. It was a striking dark blue, and it became almost black towards the centre. The rhythmic lapping against the edge of the lake lulled me into a sort of trance until all I

could see were the soft ripples and the sunlight bouncing off them. My breathing became shallow, and I desperately wanted to look away, but for some reason I felt compelled to keep staring at the water.

'Sir? Can I help you?' asked a deep, solemn voice, breaking me out of my trance.

It was the first time the butler had spoken to me since my arrival the day before.

'No, thank you,' I replied, stepping away and letting the curtains fall closed once more.

'In that case, Mr Usher wishes me to tell you that you will find him in his library,' said the butler, glaring at me.

'Thank you,' I replied, setting my teacup down on the table before hurrying out of the room, away from the butler and away from the window.

'Ah! There you are,' said Roderick as I came into his library. I noticed that he had made an effort to tidy away some of the books and instruments that had littered the floor the night before. 'I wanted to show you some of my favourite books. They are the one thing that keeps this house from feeling like a complete prison.'

As Roderick scanned the shelves and climbed up and down his library ladders, I had the chance to take in the space properly. The

night before, it had only been
lit by a solitary candle and the
fire. Now, with daylight flooding
in, I could see the room that my
friend seemed to spend most of
his time in. The windows
faced the woodlands,

and the curtains in this room were allowed to stay open. Everywhere I looked were guitars, violins and other stringed instruments. In one corner, an easel had been set up with a canvas and paints laid out nearby. Surrounding the easel were piles of painted landscapes. I moved closer to take a look and was astounded by what I saw.

CHAPTER SEVEN

'Roderick, these are very good!'
I cried, amazed at the paintings I
was looking at. Not only were they
very well painted, but they were
mostly all of the lake – the very
thing that Roderick had refused
to look at earlier. I couldn't help
but wonder again why he was so
against leaving the house.

Roderick turned to me, his arms
full of books, and his face fell a
little. 'Thank you,' he said, sadly.

'I find that painting helps to settle my mind when I get ... upset.'

'You have captured the lake perfectly,' I said. 'And this one is–' I stopped to look at a canvas that did not look like the others. It was a dark image of a long, rectangular-shaped tunnel that seemed to disappear into the earth. Strange rays of light passed

through it. It seemed much angrier than the other paintings. 'Well, this one is very interesting,' I said.

Roderick cleared his throat loudly. 'Thank you. Now, let me show you these books,' he said, ushering me away from the easel and towards the sofa in the middle of the room.

We did not talk about the paintings again that day. For the rest of the morning, we discussed our favourite books, read passages and poems out loud and talked about old times at school. I was

reminded of the boy I used to know, and we both began to feel more relaxed.

That evening, I wondered if Madeline might be joining us for dinner, but Roderick shook his head. 'Sadly, she cannot manage it,' he said. 'She had another fit this evening and has a nurse with her now. She is too weak to get out of bed.'

I felt sorry for Madeline and was scared for Roderick. To try and lift his spirits, I suggested we listen to some music. So, after dinner, we headed back up to his studio.

'You have so many fine instruments,' I said, settling myself by the fire. 'Would you play a song for me?'

'As you wish,' Roderick answered. 'But I can only play guitar as all other sounds are too much for me right now.' He took a deep breath and began to pluck and strum the strings of his guitar. He played very well, and I closed my eyes to listen and appreciate the warmth of the fire.

The song was about a house;

a beautiful, contented home and the happy family who lived there. In the first few verses, Roderick sang lightly about the sun that always seemed to shine on the house, and the many generations of families who lived happily within its walls. As the song carried on, however, the story slowly changed. The house became dark and cold, and the people in it were afraid and downcast. The last line of the song spoke of the house being lost to the water, and the people who lived there were smiling no more.

A chill ran through me, despite the fire. 'It is an old family song,' Roderick explained, putting down his guitar. 'I have heard it played all my life.'

I was about to ask him more about the meaning behind the song when the door to the library was flung open. The butler stepped inside. 'Mr Usher, you must come at once!' he cried.

Roderick knocked over his guitar, sending a tuneful crash echoing around the library as he ran towards the butler. The door slammed behind them, and I was left alone.

CHAPTER EIGHT

I did not see Roderick for the rest of the evening. At 11 p.m. I found myself yawning into the dwindling fire, so I took myself to bed in my own room. I hoped that everything was okay, but I did not want to pry.

I must have fallen asleep as the next thing I was aware of was Roderick standing over my bed, shaking me. 'Wake up!' he whispered, urgently. 'Please, please, I need your help!'

Glancing at the clock on the table, I saw that it was 3 a.m. Roderick looked dreadful. His eyes were red and puffy, and it was clear he had been crying. His hair shot off in different directions and beads of sweat had formed on his brow.

'What is it, my friend?' I gasped. 'What is the matter?'

'It is Madeline,' he cried, tears welling in his eyes and tumbling down his cheeks. 'She … she is dead!' As he said the words, Roderick fell to his knees and wept. 'She had another fit and her body was too weak to recover from it.'

I jumped out of bed and threw my arms around him. 'Roderick, I am so sorry,' I said. 'What can I do to help?'

Between sobs, Roderick looked at me. 'We must move her, quickly,' he gasped, a panicked look on his face.

'What do you mean?' I asked, confused.

'We must move her to the family tomb in the basement of the house, now,' he said. 'Before they come to take her away in the morning.'

I stood up, shaking my head in horror. 'We cannot do that,' I cried. 'What on earth would be the reason?'

Roderick also stood up and moved closer to me. His eyes darted around as though he was

tomb
A room, usually underground, where bodies are buried.

looking for spies hidden behind
the curtains. Leaning forward,
he spoke quickly and quietly.
'Madeline's condition was very
rare,' he began. 'If the doctors
take her away, they will want to
examine and study her. I cannot
let that happen. The only place
she will be safe until her funeral is
in the family tomb. No one would
dare disturb her down there!'

I sighed heavily. What Roderick said made sense. I knew that people who died of mysterious illnesses were often studied in this way, and it would break Roderick's heart for it to happen to Madeline. 'Very well,' I said, wearily, although the thought of the task ahead filled me with dread.

Chapter Nine

Madeline Usher looked as though she could have been sleeping. Her face was peaceful, and her cheeks were pink. 'Are you sure she is dead?' I whispered. 'Could the nurse have made a mistake?'

'It is certain,'

Roderick replied, beginning to cry. I felt bad for asking such a ridiculous question. 'Now, we must move her as quickly as we can.'

Carefully, the two of us carried Madeline down the many, many steps to the family tomb. It was a windowless room with carvings of angels on each wall. It felt cold and damp, and the only way in or out was through a heavy wooden door with iron hinges. An empty wooden coffin lay upon a stone plinth in the middle of the

plinth
A square block, usually of stone, on which a column or statue stands.

room, as though it were waiting for someone. We approached the coffin and gently placed Madeline inside. It was at that moment that I noticed something striking.

'My goodness, Roderick,' I said.
'You are so similar to your sister.
You look almost identical.'

Roderick gazed at Madeline
sadly. 'We are twins,' he said,

then corrected himself. 'I mean, we *were* twins. She has gone and left me all alone. My greatest fear has come true and now I must spend what time I have left grieving for my sister.'

I comforted my friend as we placed the heavy lid on the coffin and left the tomb. Slowly, we climbed the steps back up to the upper floors where our bedrooms were. I offered to sleep in Roderick's room again, but he shook his head. 'I would prefer to be on my own,' he said. 'I must get used to it from now on.'

***

I slept heavily and woke the next
morning to the sound of raised
voices. Someone was having
an argument. I dressed quickly
and rushed to see if I could
help. Roderick, who looked as
though he had not slept at all,
was standing at his front door.
A man in dark clothes stood just
outside and I could see a horse
with a black, windowless carriage
beyond him.

'What is the matter?' I asked,
standing next to Roderick.

'Tell him he can't come in,' Roderick shouted, pointing towards the man. 'I am here to take care of the young lady who has sadly passed away,' said the man, calmly. 'I am from the local undertakers. I had a call from a nurse yesterday evening who told me what had happened.'

undertaker
A person whose job is to prepare dead bodies that are going to be buried or cremated.

I placed my hands on Roderick's shoulders. 'My dear friend, let me sort this out for you. Go back inside and have something to drink. I will be there soon.'

Roderick looked between the undertaker and me, then went back into the house. I turned and smiled politely at the man. 'Forgive my friend, he has had a terrible shock and is grieving for his sister. She has been placed in the family tomb, and I believe it is the family tradition to leave her there for a week before the funeral,' I explained. 'I do hope you understand. The house is in mourning, and Mr Usher needs to be left alone with his sadness.'

The undertaker let a deep breath out. 'Of course,' he said at last. 'I will come back in a week.'

CHAPTER TEN

After Madeline's death, any
glimpse of happiness that I had
seen in Roderick had vanished.
I offered to leave him so that
he could grieve in private, but
he pleaded with me to stay.
It seemed sad that there were
no other relatives or friends
around to comfort him, so
I agreed to remain at the
House of Usher for as long
as he wanted me to.

The days were long and exhausting. Roderick flipped between silent grief and strange, wild panic. He ranted about the house, saying how he wished that he and Madeline had not been forced to take it on after their parents' deaths. 'She would be alive now if we had lived anywhere but here!' he said. 'But it was our destiny. Every generation of the Usher family has lived here. We had no choice!'

He ate very little at mealtimes and spent most of his time in the library, frantically writing in his

 journal or sleeping
on the sofa. He
had not washed
or changed his
clothes for days,
and there was
little I could say
or do to help him.

One afternoon, when Roderick
had fallen into a heavy sleep on the
sofa, I covered him with a blanket
and decided to take a walk. The
air inside the house was stuffy and
thick and I longed to stretch my
legs. A mist had formed around the
house, but it felt good to be outside.

The gardens were small, and it was clear that they had not been looked after properly for a long time. I could see that they might have once been pretty, but nothing had bloomed there for years, and the paths were overgrown with weeds. A small gate led me out to the banks of the lake and, with a slight glance back up to the house,

I decided to take a closer look.

The clear waters of the lake were even more beautiful close up. I breathed in deeply and dipped my hand into the refreshing cold water, closing my eyes. Suddenly, I heard whispering. The whispers seemed to move, as though someone were dancing around me. My eyes shot open, but there was no one there, and I could no longer hear anything. The experience unnerved me, but I put it down to the exhaustion of looking after Roderick. I tried my best to shake it off.

Dark clouds were forming in the sky. A storm was coming, and I knew I should get back inside to check on my sleeping friend. When I tried to move my feet, however, they felt heavy. I looked down, expecting to see them stuck in some kind of mud, but there was nothing there. I tried again, but I could not move. Then, a feeling that I cannot explain came over me. I felt compelled to walk towards the water. I wanted to submerge myself completely and let the water close over my head. It was as though I were terribly hungry, and the only thing that could satisfy me was to be found in the lake.

All of a sudden, thunder crashed above me, and I snapped back to my senses. Able to move my feet once more, I ran back through the gate, into the gardens and to the front of the house as quickly as I could.

Breathing heavily, I looked up at the house. The crack that I had noticed when I first arrived had become wider. In fact, it had become so large

that I could almost see daylight
peeping through the stonework
near the roof. I had to tell Roderick
that the house was no longer safe
to live in, and to tell the truth,
I wished to be away from
the place as soon as I could.

Chapter Eleven

I found Roderick by the fire in his library. The blanket I had covered him in was now wrapped around his shoulders. He looked up as I entered and smiled weakly.

'My dear friend, I think you need to leave this house at once,' I said, sitting next to him. 'I don't think it is safe!'

Roderick let out an unhappy laugh. 'That is what I have been trying to tell *you*,' he said, shrugging. 'This house killed my sister, and it will kill me too.'

He did not seem to understand what I was trying to tell him.

'I am talking about the crack!' I cried. 'There is a huge crack in the stonework, and I am afraid that the house may fall down around us.'

'Do not fear,' he said, shaking his head. 'While I am alive, the house will stay standing. It is the House of Usher. It lives and breathes along with me. It is part of me, and I am a part of it.'

There seemed to be no point arguing further, although I was

starting to feel incredibly frustrated with my friend. I understood his connection to the house and his family, especially now that he was the last Usher left, but he was putting himself in danger, and me along with him. Worse still, he no longer seemed to care what was happening to him.

I decided that I would see the week out. I could not leave while Roderick needed help with Madeline's funeral, but then I would force him to come and stay with me for a while. At least while he made repairs to the

house. Satisfied with my plan,
I went to bed.

That night, a storm raged
around the house. I woke many
times to the sound of thunder
echoing through the corridors,
and the flash of lightning
bolts outside

my window. Above the wind and rain, I heard a strange cry. At first, I thought it was Roderick, afraid of the storm, but as I listened more closely, I realised it sounded like a woman. Frightened, I clutched my bedcovers around me and tried to convince myself I was imagining things.

At breakfast the following day, Roderick did not appear in the dining room. I asked the butler where he was. 'My master is not well this morning, sir,' he said, leaving me alone.

It was still raining and, for once, I was glad that the curtains in the dining room prevented me from looking at the lake. I knew it would have swollen with the rainfall and I could not bear to see it again. I still did not understand why I had felt so compelled to walk into the water, and I did not want to think about what might

have happened had the thunder not woken me out of my trance.

The day passed by slowly. Roderick remained shut away in his room as the rain turned once again into a raging storm. Still the noises continued. A crash. A door slam. A horrifying wail. Was the house becoming more unstable or was Roderick to blame for the strange cries of anguish? My uneasiness about the state of the house increased. I could not wait to leave, but I forced a smile on my

anguish
Extreme suffering caused by mental or physical pain.

face when Roderick finally entered the library that evening. 'It is good to see you up and about,' I said.

'I am sorry for leaving you on your own all day,' Roderick replied, scratching his head. 'I have felt very tired today. I do not even know what the time is. Have you eaten dinner?'

'Yes, but I am sure the cook can make something for you if you are hungry,' I replied.

'I cannot eat,' Roderick sighed.

Thunder clapped around the library, and Roderick's eyes widened in fear.

'I'm sure the storm will pass soon,' I said, reassuringly.

'No!' Roderick cried, raising his voice. 'It will not end! Not for me!' He turned and flew out of the room.

CHAPTER TWELVE

I rushed to follow Roderick out of the library. He was heading for the dining room, which was in complete darkness. The candles had been snuffed out hours earlier when I had eaten dinner alone.

Roderick ran to the window and flung the heavy curtains aside, staring wildly out at the lake. I stood back, unwilling to go any further. That lake seemed to have strange powers, and I did not want

to be near it. 'Roderick, what are
you doing?' I asked. But he did
not answer. He stood as still as a
statue, his eyes fixed on the dark
water. I stepped a little closer.
'Come on now, my friend, let us
go back to the library and–'

'Look at it!' Roderick
demanded, his eyes still locked on
the lake. 'Look at it and tell me
there is not evil in this place!'

'Evil?' I repeated, laughing
nervously. 'It is just a storm. I am
sure when it has passed everything
will look much better.'

Roderick turned and stared

at me. His gaze was terrifying, filled with rage. 'Look. At. It!' he commanded. I swallowed heavily and slowly walked to the window. Looking down at the lake, my breath almost left my body as I took in the sight. The black water was swirling unnaturally in different directions, as though a giant were stirring the waters from above. Strange glowing lights rose up from beneath the inky waters, though what was causing them could not be seen.

'Wh– what is happening?' I whispered, full of fear.

'It is alive!' Roderick breathed.
'The lake is alive, and it knows.
It knows the house is going to fall
and soon belong to it!'

At that moment, a blood-
curdling scream echoed around
the house. I looked at Roderick,
who was trembling with fear and

shock. Again, the scream came. It was louder and more desperate than ever.

With all my strength, I grabbed Roderick's arm and pulled him to the middle of the room. He stumbled, as though waking from a dream, and looked at me

pitifully. 'Oh, my friend, what is happening to me?' Roderick cried, sobbing into my shoulder. I wished I could give him a rational explanation for what we had both just witnessed, but I could not. More than anything, I wished I could persuade him to leave the house immediately, but I knew it was useless to try before Madeline's funeral. So instead, I guided him back to the library and settled him on the sofa.

rational
Based on clear thought and reason.

A few moments of silence fell between us as we both tried to calm our nerves. Now and then, I was certain I could hear the dragging of chains or a door flying open, but when I looked at Roderick, he made no sign that he could hear anything at all. Perhaps all of the noises were in my head. The strangeness of the last few days had caused my imagination to take flight.

The crackle of the fire comforted us both, and I took down a volume of short stories from the shelf. 'Shall I read aloud?' I asked

Roderick, hoping that the sound of my voice may drown out the noises in my head. 'I think we both need a peaceful activity.'

He looked up at me gratefully. 'That sounds nice,' he replied.

I flipped through the pages of the book to a story that we both knew from our childhood. It was the story of Sir Lancelot and the dragon.

CHAPTER THIRTEEN

I cleared my throat and began the story:

'"Sir Lancelot was the most famous knight of King Arthur's round table. He was brave, bold and true. Lancelot had heard the story of a dragon hiding high up in the caves above the kingdom, so he set out to find it and kill it."'

Roderick smiled. 'I remember this story from school,' he said, closing his eyes and settling back into his chair to listen.

"'Sir Lancelot searched for many days, until he came across the entrance to a cave, with a hermit sitting outside. He asked the hermit to move, so he could slay the dragon, but the hermit would not let him in.'"

At that moment I heard a low moaning sound which frightened me more than the screaming. *It must be in my head*, I thought. I steadied my voice and carried on with the story.

"'When the hermit refused to let

Lancelot in, he pushed the hermit aside with all his might.'"

A door slammed, followed by the rattle of chains. I refused to admit that it could possibly be real.

"'Now, all that stood between Sir Lancelot and the dragon was a gigantic wooden door. Lancelot pulled out his mighty sword and charged at the door.'"

I glanced at Roderick. His eyes were tightly shut. I tried to persuade myself that it was because he was concentrating on the story, rather than because he could hear the noises too.

Desperately, I carried on reading the story.

"'Sir Lancelot burst through the gigantic door, and there stood the terrifying dragon, breathing fire!'"

Suddenly, the library door flung open with such force that it blew out every candle in the room. Only the firelight saved us from being plunged into darkness. I stared in horror as the silhouette of a strange creature appeared in the doorway. 'It cannot be!' Roderick whispered, petrified. 'It simply cannot be!'

The figure's menacing eyes were fixed on Roderick as it glided into the room. With horror, I realised I knew the creature. It was Madeline. She had risen from her tomb and was standing before us. 'Roderick! What is happening?' I cried.

'Have you not heard her? The screams and cries! The noises of her moving through the house like a demon! I tried to block them out. I tried to pretend they were not real!' Roderick pulled at his hair and rocked violently. 'She has come for me! It is time for the house to take us at last!'

Then, a realisation dawned on me – something so terrible I could hardly bear it. The noises had been Madeline, desperate to escape her tomb. She must have still been alive when we left her there. Now, she stood before

Roderick filled with rage. Her nightdress was torn and hung off her like rags. Her hands were cut and bloodied. Scratches covered her arms and legs. 'What did we do?' I asked Roderick in fear.

CHAPTER FOURTEEN

Madeline flew towards her brother, screaming with rage.

'Forgive me, sister! I did not know!' Roderick cried, holding his hands out in defence. 'It was the house! It tricked me!' Roderick tried to fight his sister off, but his frail body was no match for Madeline's anger.

As Madeline pulled at her brother's hair, scratching his face, I felt the floorboards tremble beneath me. Dust and chunks of ceiling began to fall above my head. 'We *must* leave!' I shouted, but Madeline and Roderick could not hear me. They were too focussed on each other. Every instinct screamed at me to get out of the house. I flew out of the room and down the stairs, leaving Roderick and Madeline behind me. I could hear the deafening creaking of wood and metal splitting apart as I screamed frantically: 'Get out! Get out!' I ran for the front door and threw my weight against it.

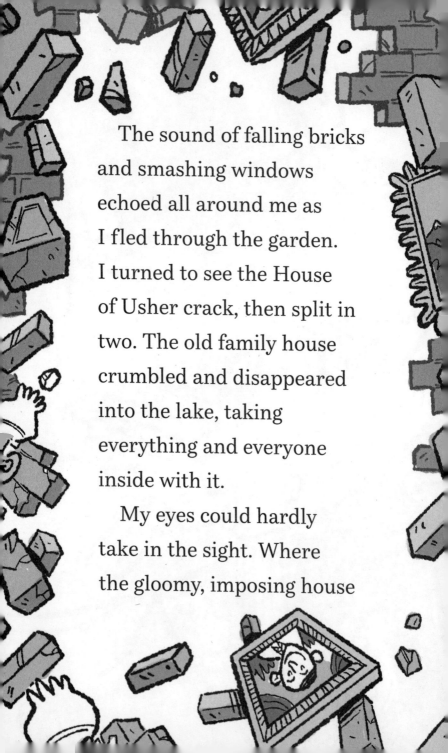

The sound of falling bricks
and smashing windows
echoed all around me as
I fled through the garden.
I turned to see the House
of Usher crack, then split in
two. The old family house
crumbled and disappeared
into the lake, taking
everything and everyone
inside with it.

My eyes could hardly
take in the sight. Where
the gloomy, imposing house

had once stood was nothing but a rising cloud of dust. Anyone who rode past from then on would see only a forest of trees and a dark lake. It was as if the house had never existed.

I let out a sob of grief for Roderick and fell to my knees. Had he known all along that this would happen? Did he just want the comfort of his old friend in his final days? It was impossible to believe, and yet,

somehow, he had known the house would be the death of him – and so it was.

***

As if out of nowhere, my horse ambled up to me, his reins loose around his neck. I fell on his strong back and mounted him gratefully, wanting to be

as far away from this place as
I could get.

Knowing that no one would
believe the fateful few days
I spent with Roderick, I wrote this
account so that someone may read
it one day and know what really
happened to the House of Usher.

EDGAR ALLAN POE

Edgar Poe was born in 1809 in Boston, USA. His father left when he was a baby, and his mother died from tuberculosis a couple of years later. Two-year-old Edgar was taken in by John and Francis Allan and became Edgar Allan Poe. Poe went on to become an author, poet, editor and literary critic. He was one of the earliest American short story writers and is considered the inventor of detective fiction.